The Wrong Overcoat

for Steve – H.O.

Text copyright © 1999 by Hiawyn Oram. Illustration copyright © 1999 by Mark Birchall
This paperback edition first published in 2003 by Andersen Press Ltd.
The rights of Hiawyn Oram and Mark Birchall to be identified as the author and illustrator of this work
have been asserted by them in accordance with the Copyright, Designs and Patents Act, 1988.
First published in Great Britain in 1999 by Andersen Press Ltd. 20 Vauxhall Bridge Road, London SW1V 2SA.
Published in Australia by Random House Australia Pty., 20 Alfred Street, Milsons Point, Sydney, NSW 2061.
All rights reserved. Colour separated in Switzerland by Photolitho AG, Zürich.
Printed and bound in Italy by Grafiche AZ, Verona.

10 9 8 7 6 5 4 3 2 1

British Library Cataloguing in Publication Data available.

ISBN 1 84270 211 4

This book has been printed on acid-free paper

The Wrong Overcoat

Written by Hiawyn Oram

Pictures by Mark Birchall

Andersen Press
London

Chimp had a new overcoat.
"It's too long," he said.
"Nonsense," said his mother. "It's just the right length."

"And the colour," he said. "I don't like this colour."

"That's a great colour," said his sister. "Everyone's wearing that colour."

"But the sleeves are too tight," said Chimp. "I can hardly move my arms."

"Then hardly move your arms," said his father. "It would be a blessing for the rest of us. Now off you go. Your friends are here."

So Chimp went off to the bowling alley with his friends, wearing his new overcoat.

"Hey, that's a cool coat," they said.

"No," said Chimp. "It's so tight I can't wear anything underneath. And it's too hot and the collar scratches."

"In fact," said Chimp, as they started bowling, "it's so hot and scratchy I've got to take it off."

"No!" said his friends. "You're not wearing anything underneath!"

So Chimp bowled in his new overcoat. As it was so long and the sleeves were so tight, he didn't bowl very well.

In fact, he bowled very badly.

"What's the matter with you?" laughed his friends.
"It's this coat," said Chimp.
"How can it be the coat?" said his friends. "That's a cool coat."

So Chimp went home feeling very low.
"I can't bowl anymore. I'm going to bed."
"You can't go to bed," said his mother. "You haven't had your tea.
And your gran's coming round to see your new coat."

So Chimp had tea with his gran in his new overcoat.

"Such nice cloth," said his gran. "Such good quality. Where'd you get him such a nice coat?"

"Allfarthings," said his mother. Chimp pricked up his ears. "That new store on Sixth Street."

So the next morning early, Chimp was on his way
to Allfarthings. As soon as the doors opened
he was up the escalator to the coat floor.

"Excuse me," he said to the assistant.

"Yes?" said the assistant.

"My mother got me a coat. But it's the wrong coat and I'd like to change it."

"Have you worn it, Sir?" said the assistant.

"I'm wearing it," said Chimp. "Which is how I know it's wrong."

"Well, we can't change it if you're wearing it," said the assistant.

"And I can't wear it if you won't change it," said Chimp.
"So I'm taking it off right now and I'm not wearing anything
underneath."

"Just a moment, Sir," said the assistant. "I'll get the manager."
And while the assistant went to get the manager up came
a kangaroo in a caftan.

"Excuse me," he said, "I couldn't help overhearing.
You're in the wrong coat."

"I am," said Chimp.

"Well, I've been trying to find a coat like yours for ages,"
said the kangaroo. "What d'you say I get the coat you want and
give it to you, and you give me your coat which is the coat I want,
we shake hands on it and go our separate ways?"

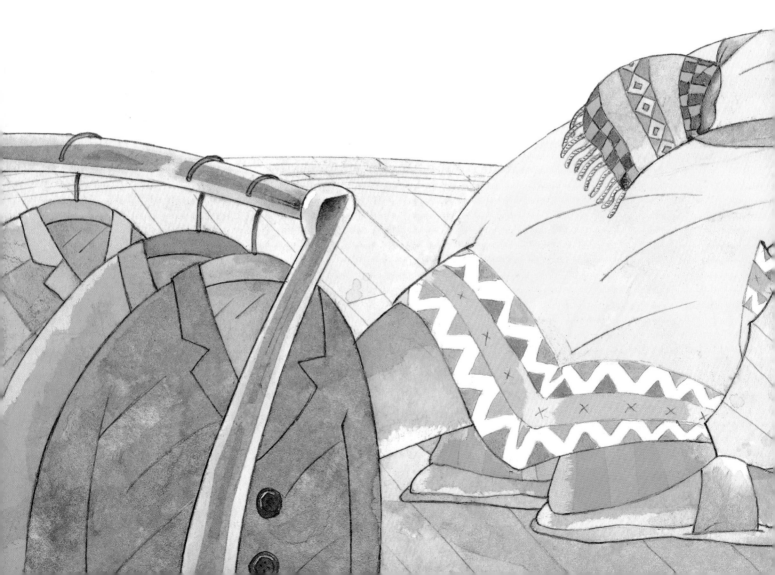

"Sounds like the first sense I've heard in days," said Chimp.

So Chimp chose a short coat in a colour that took his breath away, with lots of room to swing his arms and a velvet collar that didn't scratch. Then the kangaroo bought it,

they went into the fitting rooms, exchanged coats,
shook hands and went their separate ways.

"Well, what d'you think?" said Chimp when he got home.

"Too short," said his mother. "And not the one I gave you. I don't care for it."

"And that colour!" said his sister. "Urgh!!"

"Too much room in the arms," said his father. "You'll bowl so good in that coat you'll make enemies."

"In fact," they chorused, "altogether the wrong coat."

"For YOU!" laughed Chimp.

"And altogether the right coat FOR ME!"

More Andersen Press paperback picture books!

Ruggles
by Anne Fine and Ruth Brown

Betty's Not Well Today
by Gus Clarke

Dear Daddy
by Philippe Dupasquier

War and Peas
by Michael Foreman

Zebra's Hiccups
by David McKee

Princess Camomile Gets Her Way
by Hiawyn Oram and Susan Varley

Lazy Jack
by Tony Ross

Bear's Eggs
by Dieter and Ingrid Schubert

Rabbit's Wish
by Paul Stewart and Chris Riddell

Mr Bear and the Bear
by Frances Thomas and Ruth Brown

Frog and a Very Special Day
by Max Velthuijs

What Did I Look Like When I Was a Baby?
by Jeanne Willis and Tony Ross